JOE'S KEY UNLOCKS A DOORWAY TO TERROR. . . .

I reached up and touched the wall in Grandpa's room. It felt as gooey as pudding.

I gulped and forced myself to explore the soft area in the wall with both hands. I didn't want to touch it. It was gross. Slimy and sticky like a big, gooey sneeze.

The soft part was about as big as a doorway. I shivered. A doorway to where?

I pushed one finger into the wall. Then I shoved my hand in up to the wrist. I twisted it back and forth. The cold glop covered my skin. . . .

I slid my hand deeper into the wall inch by inch. When the goo was almost to my shoulder, my hand broke through—to the other side!

My hand was somewhere on the other side of the wall. I started to pull my hand back—and something sharp stabbed into my palm.

"Ouch!" I yanked my hand out of the wall.

I gulped as I stared down at it. On the center of my palm were two puncture marks. Teeth marks, I realized.

Something on the other side of the wall—something big—bit me!

HORROR HOTEL
PART II

R.L. Stine's
Ghosts of Fear Street® #35

HORROR HOTEL
PART II

A Parachute Press Book

A GOLD KEY PAPERBACK
Golden Books Publishing Company, Inc.
New York

This book is a work of fiction. Names, characters, places, and incidents are products of the author's imagination or used fictitiously. Any resemblance to actual events or locales or persons, living or dead, is entirely coincidental.

A GOLD KEY Paperback Original

Golden Books Publishing Company, Inc.
888 Seventh Avenue
New York, NY 10106

GHOSTS OF FEAR STREET and associated characters, slogans and logos are trademarks and/or registered trademarks of Parachute Press, Inc. Based on the GHOSTS OF FEAR STREET book series by R.L. Stine. All rights reserved, including the right to reproduce this book or portions thereof in any form whatsoever. For information address Golden Books.

Copyright © 1998 by Parachute Press, Inc.

Horror Hotel Part II written by Melinda Metz.

GOLD KEY and design are registered trademarks of Golden Books Publishing Company, Inc.

ISBN: 0-307-24907-7

First Gold Key Paperback printing October 1998

10 9 8 7 6 5 4 3 2 1

Cover art by Cliff Nielsen

Printed in the U.S.A.

HORROR HOTEL
PART II

Chapter ONE

No. No way, I thought. This can't be real.

Grandpa and I did not really switch bodies.

I squeezed my eyes shut. I'll count to three, I decided. Then I'll open my eyes and *everything will be back to normal*. I'll be standing in my bedroom, an eleven-year-old boy. And Grandpa will be standing in front of me, an old man.

"One hippopotamus," I whispered. "Two hippopotamus, three hippopotamus."

I slowly opened my eyes and peered into the mirror. My heart gave a hard thump against my ribs.

Things were definitely *not* back to normal.

I was still in Grandpa's body.

"No! No! No!" I repeated. I reached up and traced the deep lines carved in my forehead. I stroked my chin

1

and felt the prickly whiskers under my fingers. I tugged on the ends of my long gray mustache. I ran my fingers over my cheeks. My skin felt loose and rubbery.

"Hey, it's not so bad," Grandpa said. "The spell worked—mostly. It got rid of the ghost that was after you."

"Great, Grandpa," I snapped. "Now I don't have to worry about a ghost killing me. But *your* arthritis *is* killing me!"

Actually, Grandpa is right, I thought. Being in his body is bad. But it isn't nearly as bad as having a ghost after me.

Martin Jackson, a boy who died in 1864, thought I was Colin Fear—the boy who killed Martin hundreds of years ago.

It was an easy mistake to make. We had a portrait of Colin. He and I look so much alike, we could practically be twins.

Martin wanted revenge. He wanted to kill Colin. And since Colin and I look exactly alike—that meant he wanted to kill *me*.

I shuddered when I thought about how close the ghost had come. His spirit took over things in the house—everything from the bearskin rug to a houseplant—and tried to make them kill me. And when that didn't work, Martin slipped into *my* body and tried to make me walk off the roof and stab myself with a sword!

2

I thought I was doomed for sure, until Grandpa and I found a magical key under Colin Fear's portrait. Martin fought us to get the key. But Grandpa was able to beat him in the end.

Grandpa's kind of . . . unusual. He wears tinted glasses and odd clothes. And he practices magic. He's got a shelf full of old spell books—and he uses them. He says his grandmother was a Fear. Of the Fear Street Fears. The family that's famous for gruesome, ghoulish deaths.

If Grandpa's a Fear, that means *I'm* a Fear.

And the way my luck had been going lately, I was starting to believe it.

Anyway, Grandpa knew that the magic key was powerful. He used it to work one of the spells in an old book. The spell banished the ghost—and somehow made Grandpa and me switch bodies.

"Maybe if we use the key to do the spell again, we'll switch back into our own bodies," I said. "If we're the only two people in the room when we do the spell, the only way there could be a body switch is if we switch back into our *own* bodies. What do you think?"

"It can't hurt to try," Grandpa agreed. "At least I don't think it can hurt. I just have to say the spell the same way I did before."

"It *has* to work," I moaned. "I can't show up at school like this. I'm still the new kid. Everyone is

3

still deciding whether I'm cool or not! If I have to go to school in your body, no one but teachers will talk to me! And that is totally uncool."

Grandpa scratched his head, thinking. "Hey, wait a minute!" He placed his palms on top of his head and rubbed. "I've got—hair," he mumbled.

I turned toward Grandpa. He pressed his face close to the bedroom mirror. He made little fogged up circles with every breath. He looked as flipped out as I felt.

"I've *got* hair," Grandpa repeated. He combed his collar-length blond hair with his fingers.

Yeah, you've got hair. *My* hair, I thought.

"I've got *hair*!" Grandpa cried.

"Hey, I've got hair, too," I answered. I stared at my reflection. "Hair growing out of my ears!" I gave the tuft of white hair growing out of my left ear a tug. Gross.

"That's one of the things that happens when you get to be my age," Grandpa said. "At least it saves money on earmuffs."

I knew Grandpa was trying to cheer me up. But it wasn't working.

Mom and Neddy, my little brother, hurried up the stairs.

"Oh, no!" I whispered to Grandpa. "Here comes Mom! She'll flip if she finds out what happened!"

Mom stopped by my room. I tried to smile at her

4

as if everything were perfectly fine. "We're going over to the high school," she said. "The biology teacher is lending us a human skeleton for the big reopening party tonight."

The reopening! Tonight! My heart sank. I was so busy getting rid of Martin-the-ghost that I forgot all about the reopening party.

We live in a hotel—the Hotel Howie. Grandpa owns it, and we moved in so Dad could help him run it.

Business at the hotel was—well, there was no business at the hotel. So Dad came up with an idea to bring in more customers. They decided to make it the scariest place on Fear Street—like a horror movie you could sleep in. And tonight they were having a big open house to show everyone how creepy and fun the place was.

Grandpa and I have got to switch bodies before the party, I realized. Otherwise, *I'll* have to pretend to be Grandpa—in front of the whole town!

"Joe, go downstairs and eat your breakfast," Mom ordered Grandpa. "It's sitting on the stove."

Grandpa looked a little confused. "Um—all right," he said.

Mom grabbed her purse from the hall table. "We won't be gone long," she said, grabbing Neddy's hand and running back downstairs. "And, Dad, don't forget I need you to show people around at the party tonight. I found an old Dracula cape for you to wear."

Great, I thought. If I don't get my body back by tonight I'll have to play Grandpa and Dracula at the same time!

Mom and Neddy hurried out the door.

"We have to fix this as soon as possible!" I told Grandpa. "Let's do the spell now—before they get back."

"We'll do it in my room," Grandpa suggested.

"Okay," I agreed. "But I don't want Dad to hear us. The grand opening is his big thing. I don't want anything to ruin it."

Dad worked in an office on the second floor of the house. That's where he cooked up all his brilliant horror hotel-theme ideas.

I led the way down the hall to Grandpa's room. My knees creaked with every step. By the time we got there, I was huffing and puffing. "You've got to start working out," I cracked.

"See if *your* body is so much better when *you're* seventy years old," Grandpa answered as we hurried into his room.

I shut the door behind us.

Grandpa pulled the key out of his pocket. Let's chant it together, he suggested.

Please let this work, I thought. He took a deep breath and began the chant. "Change the evil for the good. Make the sun come out at night. Switch the darkness with the light."

The floor began to tremble. It's starting, I thought. It's working!

The clown painting over Grandpa's bed rattled against the wall. His thick gold rings—the ones with the magical symbols on them—fell to the floor with a clatter.

I locked my eyes on the key in Grandpa's hand and kept chanting. Only one more line to go, I thought.

I shouted out the last five words. The floor bucked under my feet and threw me to the ground.

Then the room became still and quiet.

Did it work? I needed to know.

I rubbed the back of my head. And moaned. No hair. I was still in Grandpa's body. Great. Just great. The spell didn't work.

I slowly sat up. I could feel Grandpa's bones creaking with the effort. "Grandpa, are you okay?" I asked.

Grandpa didn't answer.

"Grandpa?" My eyes darted around the small room. Searching. A shiver raced through my body as I realized the horrible truth.

Grandpa had disappeared!

Chapter TWO

"**G**randpa!" I shouted. "Grandpa, where are you?"

Okay, I told myself. Don't panic. Maybe he went downstairs without you noticing. Maybe he needed a drink of water after all that chanting.

I raced downstairs. Pain stabbed into my side. I have to slow down, I thought. I could give Grandpa's body a heart attack or something.

I checked the kitchen. No Grandpa. I checked the dining room. No Grandpa. I checked the living room. No Grandpa.

Panic rose inside me. Could the spell have backfired—again?

I lugged my creaky old body back upstairs to Dad's office. I knocked, then stuck my head inside.

8

"Do you know where Grandpa is?"

Dad finished typing a sentence on his computer. He spun his chair around and grinned at me. The kind of grin he gets when he's expecting to hear a good joke. "Yeah, I know where he is," he answered.

"Really?" I exclaimed. "Where? I need him right away!"

"He's standing right here," Dad said.

Yes! Grandpa was okay! I checked around Dad's office. But I couldn't find Grandpa anywhere.

I paused. Was Dad losing it? "Where did he go?" I asked.

"He's still standing right here." Dad frowned at me.

"Huh?" What was Dad talking about? I turned around. Even the hall was empty. And there was no one in the room but him and me. I scratched my head. My bald head.

Ugh, I thought. *I'm* Grandpa.

"Oh, yeah," I corrected myself. "I meant, have you seen Joe?"

Dad chuckled and shook his head. "Nope, haven't seen him. Sorry." He turned back to the computer. "Have you tried on that Dracula cape yet, Howie? I've got a pair of fangs you can wear tonight, if you need some. But you've probably got your own set."

Dad was totally into this horror hotel stuff. I didn't bother answering him. I just shut the door and sighed.

I guess I could tell Dad what's going on, I thought. He might believe me.

But this opening party tonight is a really big deal for him. And it's not like Dad would know how to bring Grandpa back. Even if I did tell him what was going on.

Don't give up yet. Grandpa could still be in the hotel somewhere, I told myself. I began to check the bedrooms.

I checked my room. Nothing but a pile of dirty clothes in there. No Grandpa.

He wasn't in Neddy's room, or Mom and Dad's.

I hurried to the guest wing and swung open the door to the Mummy Room. Dad's idea. Each room in the hotel had a different horror theme.

In the Mummy Room I found a stone coffin, a bedspread made of mummy-wrapping stuff, and pyramid wallpaper. But no Grandpa.

I peeked into the Vampire Room—a coffin, a bedspread made of satin coffin-lining stuff, and bat wallpaper. But no Grandpa.

I checked the Werewolf Room. Inside was a bed in a cage, a water bowl on the floor, and full-moon wallpaper. But no Grandpa.

Face it, I thought. He's gone. Poof! Just like that. Vanished. Disappeared. Bye-bye.

But how? Where?

I've got to find him somehow—before the party!

Then another horrible idea entered my mind. Grandpa's lost—in my body! How can I get my body back if it's lost forever?

Don't even think that, I told myself. Grandpa is not gone forever. And neither is my body. That *can't* happen. He has to be somewhere. And I'll find him.

I trudged back to Grandpa's room.

I'll study Grandpa's spell books, I decided. Maybe one of them says something about what to do when someone vanishes.

I bent down to pick a spell book up from the floor, then sat on the bed and started to read.

"*Joooeee,*" a voice wailed.

I jerked my head up. The room was empty. I looked out the window. No one was on the street. I opened the door and checked the hallway. No one was there either.

"*Joooeee,*" the voice wailed again.

Where was it coming from? The voice sounded so close. But I was the only one in the room.

"Grandpa?" I cried. "Is that you?"

"*Joooeee.*"

The voice, was it—was it coming from inside the wall next to Grandpa's bed?

I jumped up and pressed my ear against the wall. The wall was cold . . . and soft.

Then it began to move.

I jerked my head away. What was going on? I

backed up a step. I tensed my muscles, ready to run if I had to.

The wall stretched and bulged, forming a nose, a mouth, and eyes. A face.

My face.

"Grandpa!" I screeched. "What happened? How did you get in there?"

The lips of the face opened wide. "Help me, Joe! Help me!" Before I could say a word or move a muscle, the face disappeared. The wall snapped back to its usual shape.

Whoa! I thought. This is way too weird.

I reached up and touched the wall. My fingers shook as I ran them over the spot where the face had appeared. The wall felt as gooey as pudding.

I gulped and forced myself to explore the soft spot with both hands. I didn't want to touch it. The stuff was gross—slimy and sticky like a big, gooey sneeze.

The soft part of the wall was about as big as a doorway. I shivered. A doorway to where?

How deep is it? I wondered. If I shove my way through this pudding stuff, will I be able to find Grandpa?

I pushed one finger into the wall. Then I shoved my hand in up to my wrist. I twisted it back and forth. The cold glop covered my skin. The stuff made a wet, slurping noise.

All I could feel was the soft, cold goo. It was so cold, the bones in my hand began to ache.

I slid my hand deeper into the wall inch by inch. When the goo was almost to my shoulder, my hand broke through——to the other side!

My hand was somewhere on the other side of the wall!

I flung my hand around, trying to grab Grandpa. But I couldn't feel anything but air. I started to pull my hand back—and something sharp stabbed into my palm.

"Ouch!" I yanked my hand out of the wall.

It broke free with a big *slllurrp*!

I used my shirttail to wipe away the goo that clung to it.

I gulped as I stared down at my hand. On the center of my palm were two puncture marks.

Teeth marks, I realized. Something on the other side of the wall—something big—bit me!

Chapter THREE

I ran my fingers over the bite mark. There's some kind of animal on the other side of the wall! I thought. A big animal.

But how could that be? Mom's walk-in closet was on the other side of this wall. Wasn't it?

I hurried out of the room and over to Mom's closet door. I peeked through the slats in the wood. Was there really some kind of hungry animal lurking inside?

Too dark, I realized. I can't see anything this way. I grabbed the door handle. I took a deep breath and flung the door open.

Nothing there. Nothing inside but shelves filled with sheets and towels.

I felt the wall closest to Grandpa's room. No disgusting goo. It was completely solid.

I slowly walked back to Grandpa's room, shaking my head. This didn't make any sense. It was impossible. Totally impossible.

But I couldn't deny it. It was true. The soft spot in Grandpa's wall didn't lead to another place in the house—it led someplace *else*. Like—to some other dimension. My hand throbbed. A dimension full of dangerous animals.

I had to get Grandpa back—and fast. I didn't even want to think about what might be happening to him in that other place.

Maybe if I did the spell again, it would bring Grandpa back over to this side of the wall.

Bad idea, I decided. The spell might send me somewhere, too. Then Grandpa and I would *both* be missing. And no one would have a clue where to look for us.

I have to try *something*, I told myself. I have to find Grandpa before that thing on the other side finds him first!

I gasped. What if that thing hurt Grandpa? What if that thing hurt *my* body?

I took a deep breath. I could think of only one thing to do—go through the wall and rescue Grandpa!

I couldn't waste a second. I bolted out of the room and took the stairs as fast as I could—which felt way too slow. It would be a lot easier to save Grandpa if I didn't have to do it in *Grandpa's* body, I realized.

"Dad!" I yelled as I rushed down the hall to my father's office. "I need you—now!"

If I was going through the wall, I wanted some backup. But Dad's office was empty.

He's probably out buying creepy stuff for the party, I realized. I didn't have time to look for him.

I thought about calling my friends in the Monster Club. Nick, Robin, Johnny, and Liz. They knew everything about ghosts and monsters and other weird stuff—they wouldn't be in the club if they didn't.

Maybe one of them had investigated a case like this before. I mean, strange things like this happened all the time on Fear Street. Maybe someone else's wall had gotten soft before. Or maybe they'd seen a wall-dwelling fanged monster.

Then I realized—it would be a while before the Monster Club could get to the hotel—even if they hurried. Grandpa might not be able to wait that long.

I had to walk through. And I had to do it alone. I just had to make a few minor preparations first.

I studied myself in the mirror over Grandpa's dresser. I had on thick work gloves, a pair of goggles, a football helmet, and hiking boots. I held a flashlight in one hand. I'm ready to go in, I decided.

I tied one end of a long piece of rope around my waist. Then I tied the other end around Grandpa's bedpost. I wanted to make sure that I'd be able to find my way back to the soft spot.

I picked up my backpack and put it on backward, so that the pack was in front of me. I unzipped it and counted the baseballs inside. I planned to throw them at whatever sat on the other side, waiting to bite me.

I had ten balls. I hoped that was enough.

I marched over to the wall. I took a deep breath— and pushed my foot into the soft spot. It didn't seem as soft as when I stuck my hand through.

I poked one of my fingers into the wall. Yeah. The spot in the wall was definitely thicker. It felt more like wet rubber cement than pudding now.

It's hardening up, I realized.

Then I had a terrifying thought. What if it hardens up completely while I'm on the other side? What if Grandpa and I get trapped in the wall forever!

Chapter FOUR

"**D**on't worry, Grandpa, I thought. I'm coming to get you!

Knock, knock, knock. I spun around. Who was at the door?

"Dad, I need you downstairs," Mom called from outside the bedroom. "People are going to start arriving for the party soon."

Ugh! That stupid party!

I couldn't take the time to help Mom now. The wall could be totally hard by the time I got back upstairs. Grandpa—and *my* body—would be lost forever.

"Uh, I'm . . . not feeling well," I called back. I gave a loud cough.

"That excuse didn't work on *you* when I was a kid

and wanted to stay home from school," Mom answered. "And it's not going to work on *me* now."

She swung open the door and frowned at me. "What are you wearing?"

"The question is, what are *you* wearing?" I nearly choked on my laughter. Mom's hair was hidden under a huge, teased-up black wig. The wig had streaks of white running through either side of it. Like lightning bolts. Mom wore a long silver-colored gown and had small bolts sticking out of her neck.

"You know I'm playing the bride of Frankenstein for the party," Mom stated. "I thought *you* were going to be Dracula. So what's with that costume?"

I drummed my fingers on the football helmet as I struggled to come up with an answer. "It's not a costume. I put this stuff on because—I think I have a chill!" I burst out. "I told you I was feeling sick. I put on the helmet to keep my head warm. And the gloves to keep my hands warm."

"And the goggles?" Mom asked.

"I'm so sick, even my eyeballs feel cold," I lied.

"Should I ask why you tied yourself to the bed?" Mom said.

"Um, I'm dizzy," I said. "I was afraid I'd faint and fall over."

Mom shook her head. "Dad, come on. You know how important tonight is. I know dressing up like this feels silly, but if we don't start bringing in more business, we could lose the hotel."

Whoa. I knew things weren't great. I knew we really hadn't been getting any guests. But I didn't know there was a chance we would *lose* the hotel. Where would we live? Would we still stay in Shadyside?

I did *not* want to have to be the new kid at some other school. I wasn't an old kid at this one yet. And I was just starting to make some cool friends. I just got into the Monster Club!

"Don't you have anything to say?" Mom sounded really upset, and I felt bad. But I couldn't change my mind. My body—and Grandpa—could be getting mauled right now.

"But I might be contagious," I said. I had a story and I was sticking to it. "It would be bad for business if I made all the people at the party sick, too."

"If you can look me in the eye and tell me you're really sick, I'll try to handle things myself," Mom said.

Oh, man. Not the look-me-in-the-eye test, I thought. I always flunked that one.

"Okay, I'll be downstairs in one minute," I muttered. I pulled off the football helmet, the goggles, and the gloves.

"Good," Mom answered. "I left your Dracula cape hanging on the hall coat rack." She hurried out the door. *Thunk*! She bumped the top of her wig against the doorframe.

I unfastened myself from the bedpost and followed Mom downstairs. I grabbed the cape and tried to tie it around my neck.

Ow! Grandpa's fingers were hard to bend. And they hurt! Great, I thought. Now I have to deal with arthritis, too.

Mom bustled into the hall. "Dad, before you put that cape on, would you run to the store and get me some ice?" Mom asked. "I need four big bags."

"Okay." I wondered how Grandpa's legs would do pedaling my bike. All that bending and straightening might hurt a lot.

"Take my car," Mom said. "It's more reliable than that thing you drive." She thrust the car keys into my hand.

I stared at the keys. *Drive?* I'm supposed to *drive*? I thought.

Mom gave me a little shove. "Come on, Dad!" she scolded. "Hurry!"

I wanted to tell Mom I didn't know how to drive. But how could I explain that? I don't think you can just forget how once you've learned.

I walked out to the car and slid into the driver's seat. The keys jingled in my hand. This won't be any problem, I told myself. I've seen adults drive a million times. And I always win on the race car video game in the mall. My initials are all over the list of top scores.

Okay, step one—turn on the engine, I thought. I looked at the keys on my mother's key ring. Which one was the right one?

I tried the first key. It wouldn't fit. It must be for the trunk, I thought. I tried the next one. It slid in easily. I turned the key, and heard the low purr of the engine.

Step two—put the car in reverse, I coached myself. I pulled the gearshift down to "R." Step three—give it some gas.

I shoved my foot down on the gas pedal. The car lurched down the driveway. Hey, look at me—I'm driving! I thought. I'm doing it!

I gave the car a little more gas. Whoa! It zoomed into the street. Turn the wheel, turn the wheel! I screamed at myself.

I backed into the street, yanking the steering wheel to the right. The car sputtered.

Needs more gas, I figured. I pressed my foot on the gas pedal.

Zoom! The car bolted into the street—backward. Straight toward Mrs. Crandel's mailbox!

I jerked my foot off the gas pedal and slammed down on the brake.

The car jolted to a stop—two inches from the mailbox.

That was too close, I thought, catching my breath. Way too close. I could have knocked that mailbox totally flat!

It was kind of scary, controlling a ton of metal.

Okay, the gas is on the right and the brake's on the left, I muttered to myself. And I'm parked in the middle of the street. I can't sit here blocking traffic.

I slid the car into drive and headed down the street. I flipped on the radio. This was extra cool. I could listen to whatever I wanted. And I could listen to it as loud as I wanted.

I turned the volume knob all the way to the right. I started tapping my foot to the music, and the car shot forward.

Stop sign, I told myself. Stop sign! But the message didn't get from my brain to my foot fast enough. I raced past the sign—heading straight toward a purple truck!

I was going to crash!

Chapter FIVE

Brakes! I thought. Brakes! Now!

But my foot felt frozen on the gas pedal. "Nooo!" I screamed. "I'm going to hit it!"

I jerked the wheel to the right as hard as I could. The brakes squealed as the car swerved out of the path of the purple truck.

I pulled the car over to the curb. My hands shook so hard, I could hardly hold on to the wheel. If I had turned one second later . . .

I squeezed my eyes shut. I could almost hear the crunch as Mom's car slammed into the truck.

That didn't happen, I told myself. You're okay. The truck is okay. The truck driver is okay. Everything is okay.

I snapped off the radio. I wasn't ready to do two

things at once. Driving was hard enough by itself.

I took a deep breath. I turned my head to see if it was safe to pull back out into the street. The stiff muscles in my neck cracked.

All clear, I thought. I pressed down lightly on the gas pedal and started down the street.

A red convertible sped past me. "Hey, Grandpa," the driver yelled. "The speed limit is thirty, not three."

I'm not Grandpa, I thought. I'm just a kid!

I didn't speed up. This time I was taking it slow.

"Here you go." I handed the last party guest her coat and practically pushed her out the door. It had been more than three hours since I checked the spot in the wall. It could be totally hard by now.

I ran up the stairs to Grandpa's room.

"Dad," Mom called.

I was starting to get used to being called that. Mom had kept me running the whole party. Dad, get some ice. Dad, put on the cape and scare the people in the Dracula Room. Dad, pass around the punch. What did she want now? I really had to get upstairs to the hole.

I slowly turned to face her. "I just wanted to say thanks. I couldn't have handled the party without you."

"You're welcome," I said. Then I continued up the

stairs. I took them two at a time. Pain jabbed into my knees, but I didn't slow down. I couldn't let Grandpa's body keep me from moving fast. Not now.

I pulled on the gloves, the football helmet, the goggles, and the backpack full of baseballs. I grabbed my flashlight and tied myself to the bedpost.

Then I took the first step into the wall. It *had* hardened up during the last three hours. It felt more like peanut butter than wet rubber cement now. But I could still fight my way through.

The unnatural cold of the goo numbed my legs. I felt its wet stickiness envelop me.

I took another step. This time the goo surrounded my head. The flesh on my scalp crawled from the feel of it. It smeared across my goggles, blinding me. It slimed every inch of my skin and hair.

I held my breath and struggled forward. The ice cold goo filled my nose and mouth, stinging me. My head felt like bursting from the pressure.

I struggled to take a breath—and pulled more goo into my mouth and nose.

No! I thought. I can't breathe!

Chapter SIX

My lungs began to burn. My heart hammered against my ribs.

Just keep going, I ordered myself. I staggered forward, forcing my legs through the goo.

Red dots exploded in front of my eyes. My lungs felt ready to burst. I couldn't do it. I couldn't make it to the other side. I'd never be able to find Grandpa!

I hurled myself forward with all my strength—and stumbled out—into freezing air.

I made it! I was on the other side!

Ptew! I spit out the awful goo that filled my mouth. I sucked in a big gulp of air, then another.

I yanked off the goo-covered goggles and stared around. I seemed to be standing in a long, dark tunnel.

I clicked on the flashlight and shined it around the

tunnel. Deep holes about as big around as pizzas covered the walls. No sign of Grandpa anywhere.

"Grandpa?" I called.

Nothing. Only an echo.

I have to find Grandpa fast, I thought. If that spot hardens up entirely, we'll both be stuck here forever. I checked the knot on the rope around my waist. Still tight. I started forward.

A clicking noise sounded from somewhere on the floor. I felt something brush against the leg of my jeans. I froze. What was that?

When I glanced down, I saw nothing.

Whatever it was, it was fast. It was gone before I could even see it.

Good, I thought. I don't want to see it. I don't want to deal with it. I just want to find Grandpa and *get out* of here.

I continued down the tunnel. My footsteps echoed against the stone floor. This place is mega-creepy, I thought.

I swung the flashlight back and forth in front of me, letting the beam hit as much of the tunnel as possible. I didn't want anything jumping out at me.

The light caught something in one of the pizza-sized holes. Something sparkling. "What's that?" I asked out loud. I took a step closer to get a better look.

It's a necklace, I realized. The hair on the back of my neck stood up. How did that get in there? I wondered. And what happened to the person it belonged to?

I shined the flashlight into the next hole. I saw a neon-pink watch. A bald baby doll lay in the next hole.

I checked another hole and gasped. I couldn't stop staring at the high-top sneaker that rested inside. It was the same sneaker Grandpa had been wearing when he disappeared. *My* sneaker.

"Grandpa," I shouted. "Grandpa, where are you?"

I listened hard, hoping Grandpa would answer. But all I heard was a soft clicking sound. It seemed to be coming from inside the hole. I peeked in even farther.

A pair of bright silver eyes appeared in the darkness behind the sneaker.

I stumbled back. What was in there?

The clicking sound grew louder. It sounded as if it were coming from all around me. I turned. A pair of eyes appeared in each of the holes that lined the tunnel.

I reached into my backpack and pulled out a baseball. I held it over my head. "You things stay away from me. Just stay in your little holes or I'll have to use this," I shouted.

I concentrated on sounding like a tough guy. But my voice cracked.

Great. I sound like a total wimp. Why don't I just invite those things to come and get me?

I turned and took off farther down the tunnel. Grandpa's body couldn't take running for very long. I started huffing and puffing right away, but I didn't slow down.

I saw a faint glow in the distance. The tunnel must end up ahead, I thought. Maybe Grandpa is there waiting for me. He'd be crazy to stay in here with those . . . *things*.

Whatever they were.

I forced myself to speed up. My knees creaked and popped with each step. And I wheezed with each breath.

Almost there, I told myself. I could see the opening at the end of the tunnel now.

I raced forward—then skidded to a stop.

The mouth of the tunnel was covered by a huge spiderweb. It stretched from top to bottom and side to side. It covered every inch of the opening.

I swallowed hard. How big was the spider that made that web?

And where was the spider now? If I tried to break through the web, would it get me?

I heard a muffled moan coming from the web. I jerked my head toward the sound.

Something was trapped in the web. Something wrapped in a tight cocoon of the spider's thread. Something the size and shape of a kid's body!

No! No, it couldn't be!

I raced over. I saw a pair of brown eyes staring up at me through layers and layers of webbing.

My eyes.

"Grandpa!" I cried.

I reached out to tear Grandpa free. *Please be alive*, I prayed. *Please don't be dead.*

Then I heard it again . . . *click click click click*. It was coming from behind me. As I turned it grew louder.

Click, Click, Click, Click CLICK CLICK CLICK CLICK . . .

My heart started pounding double time.

Spiders! As big as cats! Crawling down the tunnel toward me!

I glanced behind me at the web. No place to run. The huge spiders formed a quivering half circle around me.

I was trapped.

Their silver eyes glistened as they stared at me. Their long black teeth gnashed together.

Their tiny feet clicked on the stone floor. *Click, click, click . . .*

The spiders inched closer and closer.

I gasped.

They were going to attack!

Chapter SEVEN

Nine gigantic spiders surrounded me. Giant spiders with teeth! And lots of fuzzy black legs.

I gripped a baseball in my hand. Nine spiders. And I had ten baseballs. I had to make every throw count.

My arm shook as I pulled it back. I took aim at the closest spider.

I hurled the ball as hard as I could.

Ooof! I grunted. The ball landed just a few feet in front of me. Pain exploded in my shoulder.

Oww! Grandpa's arm was really stiff.

The spiders scuttled closer, their teeth clicking.

Nine baseballs left. I can't miss again.

I grabbed another ball. You can do this, I coached myself. Concentrate.

I threw the ball. Pain blasted through me again.

But this time I hit my target.

Splat! The closest spider exploded, spraying green goo onto my shoes.

Whoa! Bringing the baseballs with me was the best idea I ever had. They worked better than hand grenades.

"Ha! You spiders are in trouble now!" I yelled.

I grabbed another ball and threw it. This time, completely ignoring the pain.

Splat! Each of the spider's eight legs flew in a different direction.

"Direct hit!" I shouted.

Two of the spiders scuttled away. "That's right, run!" I yelled after them.

I can beat them, I thought. I'm going to do it!

I'll crush these spiders. Then I'll save Grandpa and get out of here!

I grabbed another ball. *Wham! Splat!*

"Another one down! Yes!" I yelled. I pumped my fist into the air.

Only four spiders left. I took aim at one of them.

Before I could react, it scurried forward—and shot a long web at my eyes.

"Aaah!" I dropped the baseball and brushed the web off my face. It stuck to me like chewed bubble gum.

I grabbed for another ball. Two of the spiders began to circle me.

What are they up to? I wondered.

I whirled around, trying to keep track of them as they circled me. *Zap!* Long, sticky webs bound up my legs.

They're trying to trap me! I realized in a panic. They won't let me move!

I tried to kick free of the webs, but they were too tight. They held my legs glued together.

"No!" I screamed. "I won't let you get me!"

My heart thundered in my ears. I had to do something fast. I shot a ball at the nearest spider.

Crack! It smacked the spider in the leg, breaking it off its body. Green muck poured out of the severed stump. It gave a high-pitched squeal and hobbled away.

"Three to go," I muttered. I pulled my arm back. One of the spiders shot a web at the ball and yanked it out of my hand.

Huh? I stared at my empty fingers.

I scowled and grabbed another ball from my backpack. As the spider reeled in the first ball, I fired another. *Splat!*

Two to go, I thought. Only two.

I reached into my backpack. Thick, sticky webs pinned one arm to my side.

"No!" I grunted. I strained to free my right arm. Too late! It was stuck!

My heart pounded. In a few seconds the spiders could have me wrapped in webs from head to toe!

I still have my left hand, I thought. I grabbed a baseball and slammed it down at one of the spiders.

It missed.

The spiders shot webs at my left hand. "No!" I screamed. I twisted out of the way. Needles of pain jabbed into my back and neck. Grandpa's sore back! I fought hard to ignore it.

I grabbed another ball. Then I took a deep breath. Focus, I told myself. You can't miss. Not now.

I pictured a target on the back of the closest spider, and threw the ball with all my strength. *Splat!*

"It's down to you and me," I yelled at the last spider.

I stuck my hand into the backpack.

Empty!

I used all the baseballs.

I was doomed.

The spider shot a web at my left hand and glued it to the backpack. The next web sealed my lips shut. I couldn't even scream.

In two seconds I was going to look like a mummy. And I would be powerless to fight the spiders.

I'd be a spider snack!

No! That was not going to happen.

I aimed my body at the spider, and fell forward.

I hit the hard floor of the tunnel.

Splat! The spider was flattened beneath me. His green spider guts spattered all over me.

In my face and my hair—everywhere.

My stomach lurched.

I couldn't think about how grossed out I was. There was no time. I had to get out of these webs and get Grandpa!

I rolled off the squashed spider. Then I rocked myself from side to side using the rough stone floor to tear open the webs.

When Grandpa gets his body back, he's not going to thank me for this, I thought. He's going to be a walking, talking bruise. I could feel the stone floor working. I rocked harder. As soon as I could move my arms, I ripped the rest of the webs off me.

Part of me wanted to curl up in a little ball right there on the floor. My body shook with exhaustion. Pain stabbed into every muscle. My bones ached. Even the few wisps of hair on my head felt tender.

But the wall! It was getting harder every second! I couldn't take time to rest. I shoved myself to my feet and staggered over to the web. I ripped Grandpa free.

He fell to the ground and lay still.

Oh, no. Am I too late? I thought.

"Grandpa, are you okay?" I cried. "Please, please, please be okay."

I pressed my ear to Grandpa's chest. I couldn't hear him breathing.

I used my fingers to scrub the webs off Grandpa's

lips and nose. "Come on, Grandpa. Breathe!" I begged.

Grandpa coughed and sputtered. I reached into his mouth and pulled out a long rope of gray spider-web.

Ugh—*gross*! I thought.

"I'm all right," Grandpa said. His voice sounded dry and scratchy.

"Then let's get out of here." I helped Grandpa up, and the two of us headed back down the tunnel.

Sweat dripped down my back and neck. It slid down my forehead and into my eyes. But I forced Grandpa's old legs to keep pumping.

We dashed to the end of the tunnel. I turned to Grandpa. "Grab hold of this rope," I said. "I tied it to your bed. You can use it to guide you to the other side."

I pushed Grandpa into the wall. He gave a high yelp of pain. "It's as hard as a rock," he cried. "We'll never get through!

"Joe, I think we're stuck here!"

Chapter EIGHT

I shoved the wall with both hands. It felt totally solid.

I yanked the football helmet off my head and thrust it at Grandpa. "Use this—smash open the wall!" I cried.

No way could I do it myself.

In fact, I realized, I could hardly stand up. My legs were trembling. My arms felt too heavy to lift. My lungs ached with every breath.

Grandpa smashed the helmet against the wall. A long crack appeared in the surface.

"It's working!" I cried. My voice sounded soft and scratchy. "Keep going!"

Grandpa slammed the helmet down again. Another crack appeared.

"Try taking a running start," I suggested. I hated just standing there. I wanted to *do* something. But I had used up all my old body's strength and energy.

Grandpa backed up a few steps. Then he charged at the wall. He rammed the helmet into it.

A loud cracking sound echoed through the tunnel. Pieces of stone crumbled and fell to the floor.

I glanced into the hole Grandpa made. Score! I could see a layer of the soft orange goo.

I touched it. It still had that hideous cold feeling. But now it felt as hard as clay.

"We can tunnel out!" I yelled at Grandpa. "Dig!"

Grandpa crouched next to the hole and started shoveling out the hardened goo with his hands. I knelt beside him and scooped out a few handfuls.

"This stuff is freezing," Grandpa exclaimed.

"Yeah, my hands are already numb," I agreed. At least I can't feel how much they hurt, I thought.

Click, click, click.

"Did you hear that?" Grandpa yelped.

Click, click, click.

I took a deep breath and glanced over my shoulder. It was dark in the tunnel. But I could see silver eyes—moving closer.

More spiders! And I'm out of baseballs, I remembered.

"Hurry, Grandpa!" I yelled. "Get us out of here!"

I turned back to the wall and scooped out goo with both hands.

Click, click, click.

My stomach clenched. They'll be in web-shooting range any second, I thought.

"We're almost out!" Grandpa told me. "Just a couple of feet of digging to go. You go in first. I'll try to hold the spiders off."

"No," I said. "You're smaller. You'll dig faster."

I untied the rope from my waist and handed the end to Grandpa. "Use this to pull you along," I instructed. "Do it! Go!"

Grandpa grabbed the rope and slithered into the hole.

Click, click, click.

I spun around and faced the spiders. One of them shot a web at me. It landed a few inches from my foot.

"Stay away from me!" I screamed. I threw the foot-ball helmet at the spiders. They scuttled backward. But only a few steps.

I checked the hole. Grandpa was deep inside. All I could see were his feet.

Click, click, click.

The spiders advanced on me.

I dove into the hole. "Push!" I told Grandpa. "Push through the rest of the way!"

I grabbed Grandpa's ankles and held on as tight as I could. I wished his fingers would bend more.

The goo plopped down onto my shirt and pants. The cold numbed my body. I felt myself moving. Grandpa was doing it! He was pushing through!

Suddenly, I felt myself falling. I landed on something soft and fuzzy.

I opened my eyes. Blue carpet—all around me.

Yes! I was back in Grandpa's room! Grandpa lay on the floor next to me—covered from head to toe in orange goo.

"We're back!" I exclaimed.

"We're back!" Grandpa repeated. "Woo hoo!"

I slowly sat up. "Ouch," I muttered. I hauled my creaky old body to its feet. I ran my hands over the soft spot on the wall.

It was hardening up fast. Soon it would disappear totally, I hoped.

I thought about what lived on the other side—and shuddered.

I heard a knock on the door. "Dad?" Mom called. "I wanted to tell you the good news. We've got reservations for the Dracula Room *and* the Mummy Room. The party really was a great way to get some new business."

"The party's over? It already happened?" Grandpa exclaimed.

Mom swung open the door. "Yes, Joe, it's over. And where have *you* been hiding? I was hoping you'd be around to help us."

Uh-oh. I was in trouble. And Grandpa wasn't making things any better. He wasn't even answering. He just stared at Mom with his mouth hanging open.

"There was a, um, concert at Joe's school," I jumped in. My mother liked things that sounded educational. "I thought it was important for him to go, so I gave him permission."

That sounded good, I thought. Very adult.

"I wish one of you had told me," Mom said. But I could tell she wasn't mad at me anymore.

"Sorry," Grandpa mumbled.

I didn't know if he was answering as me or as himself. But it didn't matter. What he said worked for both of us.

"It's late. You should head to bed, Joe," Mom said. "See you both in the morning." I heard her walk away.

"Sorry, kiddo. I'm not used to being called Joe," Grandpa explained. "I messed up."

I shrugged it off. "What *happened* to you?" I asked. "How did you end up—" I gestured toward the wall—"wherever that was?"

Grandpa shook his head. "It's like some other dimension or something. As soon as we said the last word of the spell, I just found myself there. I didn't know where I was. My eyes were still getting used to the dark, when those spiders attacked me."

I shuddered. Poor Grandpa! Attacked by giant spiders—*in the dark*!

"Do you think the hole will ever open up again?" I asked. I glanced over at Grandpa's wall. It looked perfectly normal now.

"I hope not," Grandpa answered. "But I don't know how it got there in the first place, so it's hard to be sure."

I had a bunch more questions, but I was too tired to ask them. I yawned. "I think I *will* go to bed. I'm so exhausted I can hardly stand up."

"Me, too. I guess I'll head down to your room. See, I'm already starting to remember who I'm supposed to be." He stood up and shuffled over to the door.

"I hope we won't have to remember for long," I answered. "I have to go to school on Monday, you know. And we're having fitness tests in gym! Sorry, Grandpa, but I'll never pass the tests in this body. We've got to switch back as soon as possible!"

"We'll go through the spell books first thing tomorrow," Grandpa promised. "I need my body back, too, you know. I'd look pretty funny playing bingo looking like this." He gave me a little wave as he left the room.

I stood up and trudged into the bathroom. That was one good thing about being Grandpa—he had a bathroom all to himself. He didn't have to share with Neddy.

The first thing I wanted to do was brush my teeth. I could still taste traces of the orange goo in my mouth. And I wanted to get rid of every last bit of it.

I grabbed the toothbrush out of the holder. It felt a little strange to be using someone else's toothbrush. But, hey, I was using someone else's teeth, too.

I squeezed on some toothpaste and started to brush.

My teeth *wiggled*.

Whoa, being old sure is weird, I thought. Wiggling teeth! *Gross me out*.

I gave my teeth another couple brushes. They definitely felt loose. What's going on? I wondered.

I stared into the mirror. My teeth looked okay. And I didn't see any blood or anything.

I shook my head.

Ker-plunk!

My teeth fell into the sink!

Chapter NINE

"**A**aah!" I yelled.

Grandpa's teeth! I made them all fall out!

I stared into the sink. The teeth lay inside—smiling up at me.

Oh, man. How am I going to tell Grandpa about this? I wouldn't like it if he trashed *my* body while he's using it.

I peered into the sink again. Hey, wait! The teeth are all still stuck together. That's weird.

I reached down and picked up the teeth. They're fake! I realized. Dentures!

I laughed. I didn't know Grandpa wore dentures.

I bet I'm the only eleven-year-old who sleeps with his teeth in a glass, I thought.

"I should have told you about the dentures," Grandpa said the next morning. We were sitting on his bed in his room. The room I'd slept in the night before.

"It was kind of freaky when they fell out," I admitted. "But I decided to pretend I was a hockey player. Half of them have had their teeth knocked out. Besides, it's not like it's the *worst* thing that happened to me yesterday."

"Well, today is going to be much better," Grandpa told me. "One of these books will have to have a spell we can use to switch our bodies back."

He grabbed one of the spell books from the shelf over his bed and stretched out on the floor. He began flipping through the pages.

I stared at the books piled up on the shelf and sighed. There had to be at least a hundred of them.

Good thing it's Sunday, I thought. It might take all day to check through these.

I chose a thick green book off the top of the pile. I tried to sit on the floor next to Grandpa. Ouch! Grandpa's legs just didn't bend that way.

I slowly lowered myself into Grandpa's over-stuffed armchair instead. I can't wait until I can *move* again, I thought.

The book's cover creaked as I opened it. The pages were charred around the edges, and they smelled like smoke.

"How old are these books anyway?" I asked.

Grandpa glanced over. "I think that one came from Simon Fear's library. A few volumes survived the fire, and my grandmother somehow got her hands on them. She was a cousin of Simon's, so you and I have a little Fear blood in us."

The remains of the old Fear mansion stood down the street from the hotel. My friend Nick, from the Monster Club, said it was haunted. It probably was, too. It gave me the creeps.

"Are the stories about Simon Fear true?" I asked. "I heard he talked to ghosts. And that he practiced some kind of weird magic to turn people into zombies and stuff."

"He was a strange man," Grandpa answered. "And a powerful one. The most powerful man in Shadyside."

Grandpa hesitated. "Some people think he used a kind of dark magic to get his power. Maybe they are right. Or maybe old Simon was just lucky."

I turned to the first spell in the book. "To Call the Dead from Their Graves," I read aloud.

I imagined all the caskets in the Fear Street Cemetery swinging open. The corpses clawing their way to the surface—and staggering toward my house.

No thanks, I thought. I quickly turned the page.

The next spell was "To Summon the Bees from

Their Hives." An illustration showed a woman covered from head to toe with bees. Her mouth hung open in a scream. More bees were crawling on her tongue.

I swallowed hard. I turned the pages faster. I saw a spell for turning someone's blood to sand, and a spell for creating a hurricane.

But I didn't find a spell for switching bodies.

I set the book on the floor by my chair and took another book from the pile. It was called *The Secrets of the Power*. Maybe this one will have the spell we need, I thought.

I tried to open the book, but the pages were stuck together. "Somebody must have spilled something on this one," I muttered.

I gently pulled the first page away from the others. I tried to read the spell. But a rust-colored stain covered the page.

It's blood, I realized. I shuddered. This book is covered in blood!

I slammed the book shut and threw it on the bed.

I wished we could throw all of the books away. I hated even being in the same room with them.

But the secret to getting my body back is in one of these books, I reminded myself. I can't wimp out now.

I reached for a pale blue book near the bottom of the heap. It didn't look too bad.

"I found it!" Grandpa exclaimed. "I found the spell

we need." He jumped up and hurried over to me. "Let's try it."

I pushed myself to my feet. "Okay, let's do it."

Grandpa pulled the key out of his pocket. "First we need the key—the power that makes the magic work."

"Hold it. Maybe we should try the spell without the key," I suggested. "Our spells have been getting all messed up. Maybe the key is causing it."

Grandpa shook his head. "The magic won't work without the key. Chanting the spells is important. But the key gives us power."

I sighed. "The key had power, all right. The power to make everything even worse than before!"

"I've tried these spells before—and they never worked until I found the key," Grandpa pointed out.

I gave in. "Then I guess we have to use it."

Grandpa nodded. He motioned to me to begin. I grabbed one end of the key. We started chanting the spell in the book. Nothing is happening, I thought.

The floor isn't trembling. The sky isn't darkening.

Maybe that's not how this spell works, I told myself.

I kept chanting. Still nothing changed. I was going to be stuck in this body forever!

Grandpa and I chanted the last word of the spell. We stared at each other. "It didn't—"

I stopped short.

My body started tingling. I felt as if I were getting zapped by a hundred electric buzzers at once.

My skin felt hot. I stared down at my hands. They turned from light pink to dark pink to red!

The smell of hot dogs cooking on a grill hit my nose.

No, not hot dogs, I realized. It's *me*.

The spell—it's baking me alive!

Chapter TEN

My skin was burning! The edges of my fingers turned black.

My blood felt like lava as it raced through my veins. Every beat of my heart sent fire through my body.

Water!

I dashed into the bathroom and jumped into the shower. I turned on the cold water full blast.

Smoke rose off my body as water seeped through my clothes and ran over me. I tilted my head back and let the water run down my throat.

The icy water cooled me inside and out. "Aaah," I sighed. Then I thought of Grandpa.

"You have to get in here," I yelled. I raced out of the shower. My feet squeaked on the tile floor.

I yanked open the bathroom door. The smell of burning hair and skin hit my nose. My stomach turned over.

I grabbed Grandpa by the arm and dragged him into the bathroom. I shoved him under the shower spray.

A sizzling sound met my ears as the water hit Grandpa's skin.

"Woo-hoo! I'm staying in here forever," Grandpa cried. "This feels so good."

I leaned against the bathroom wall. My legs felt so weak. That was intense, I thought.

I closed my eyes. My wet clothes felt good against my skin. But I'm making a major puddle on the floor, I thought. I better wipe it up or Mom will have a fit.

I pushed myself away from the wall and headed for the towel rack. I caught sight of my face in the medicine cabinet mirror. I gasped.

Fat white blisters covered my forehead and cheeks and nose. Even my lips had blisters.

I glanced down at my hands. They had the blisters, too.

I pulled my wet shirt up and checked my stomach. More blisters!

I touched one of the blisters on my nose—and it popped. The skin underneath looked smooth and healthy. Hmmm. That's weird.

Popping the blister didn't hurt or anything, so I popped another one. The skin underneath the blister wasn't burned or red. Cool!

I grabbed a towel and scrubbed my face with it. I could feel the blisters popping under the rough material.

I think I got them all, I thought. I lowered the towel. No. No way. This can't be real.

"Grandpa!" I screamed. "You have to see this."

Grandpa shut off the water and stumbled out of the shower. Blisters covered him, too. "What? What's wrong?" he exclaimed.

"Look at my face!" I cried.

Grandpa's mouth fell open. "The spell worked!"

"I have my own face back!" I shuffled around the room, doing a little victory dance. Then I handed Grandpa a towel. "All you have to do is pop the blisters."

I rubbed the top of my head with both hands. The blisters popped. And under the blisters was hair. Thick blond hair.

"I've got hair!" I exclaimed.

Grandpa gave his head a few more rubs. "I've got hair, too—hair growing out of my ears."

"Yes!" I gave Grandpa a high five. "We're back!"

My Monster-Club friend Nick dribbled a basketball into my kitchen. "Ready to lose?" he asked.

"No way. I'm feeling lucky today," I answered. I smiled at Grandpa as I followed Nick out the side door. I was totally ready to play some one-on-one.

Nick ran over to the driveway and tried to sink one from the sidewalk. He missed.

I grabbed the ball and dribbled toward the basket. "Look out. Here comes the famous Turner slam dunk."

I jumped as high as I could and bounced the ball off the rim.

"You're too short to dunk," Nick said. He grabbed the ball and tried to spin it on his finger.

"Hey, I'm taller than you," I shot back. I knocked the ball away from Nick.

"No way. I'm taller," Nick bragged. He nabbed the ball and circled behind me. He shot the ball over my head. "Score!"

"Hey, wait a minute." I stopped mid-dribble. "You *are* taller."

"I told you!" Nick ran after the ball and scooped it up. "You are going *down*." Then he turned around and stared at me. "Did somebody call a time out? Because you're not moving, and I didn't hear anyone call a time out."

"You've never been taller than me before," I whispered.

"Get serious," Nick answered. "What do you think happened? You started *shrinking* or something?" He threw the ball to me.

I let the ball slip through my fingers. I heard it bounce as I turned around and headed back to the house.

"Hey! What's wrong?" Nick called. He followed me through the kitchen door.

"Game over so soon?" Grandpa called from his spot at the kitchen table. Then he studied my face. "What's wrong?" he asked.

"I want you to measure me," I said. I hurried over to the doorway leading to the dining room. That's where Dad measured all of us the first day we arrived in Shadyside. I pressed my back against the wall.

"What's going on here, Joe? You're completely freaking me out," Nick muttered.

"Come on. Measure me," I insisted.

Grandpa grabbed a pencil out of the junk drawer by the sink. He rushed over to me.

I stood beside the mark Dad had made the last time he measured me. I stretched up as straight as I could. Grandpa made a pencil mark on the wall to show how tall I was.

I spun around and checked the new mark against the old one. "I'm shrinking!" I cried. "Dad measured us all the day we moved into the hotel. That wasn't even a month ago. And today I'm an inch shorter."

"It must be your shoes or something," Nick said.

"Oh, right. I usually wear high heels," I answered.

"What if the last spell went wrong?" Grandpa said slowly. "What if. . . ?"

I shivered. "What if it makes me shrink and shrink and shrink—until there is nothing left of me at all? What if the spell is making me vanish?"

Chapter ELEVEN

"**G**ood thing your parents won't be back until late tonight. They wouldn't take this vanishing business very well," Grandpa pointed out.

I moaned and hung my head in my hands.

"Stop! Back up," Nick demanded. "What are you guys talking about?"

I looked at Grandpa. "Maybe he can help," Grandpa said.

"Okay. Sit down and get ready to hear a really weird story," I told Nick. "It all started when we cast a spell to get rid of Martin's ghost. The spell didn't work until we found a magic key. Then the spell got rid of him—but it made me and Grandpa switch bodies!"

"Whoa," Nick muttered. He said "whoa" about

twelve more times before I finished.

"Whoa is right," I said. "So, any suggestions?"

"Actually, yeah," Nick said. "I'm taking you to see Stan."

"Who's Stan?" Grandpa asked.

"Stan is . . . well, Stan is a little hard to describe," Nick said. "He's a source that we in the Monster Club use all the time. In fact, Stan is *the* source. He works at the comic book store in the mall. He can find out everything about anything."

"But how is that going to help me?" I asked.

"I'm not sure," Nick admitted. "I won't be sure until we talk to Stan."

"Stan doesn't like strangers very much," Nick said. "Wait here for a minute while I talk to him." He headed toward the front counter of the comic book store.

I picked up a comic book and pretended to read it. But I kept shooting glances at Stan. He was really tall, really tan, and really blond. He wore the brightest Hawaiian shirt I had ever seen.

I hope Nick is right about this guy, I thought. But I still found it hard to believe that Stan could do anything to help me.

I wandered over to the big window at the front of the store. I peered at my reflection. I thought I looked a little bit shorter.

How much will I shrink every hour? I wondered. Will Mom have to make me a bed in a dresser drawer tonight or what? My heart started to pound, and I turned away from my reflection.

Nick waved at me, and I hurried over to the counter.

"Hey, dude," Stan said. "Nick says you have a really big wave crashing down on you. But don't lose your mellow. I'm going to help you out. Come into my office."

Nick and I circled around the counter. We followed Stan to a door at the end of a short hallway. Stan threw open the door and ushered us inside.

I opened my mouth, then shut it again. I didn't know what to say.

Three surfboards hung from the ceiling. Plastic sea gulls perched on each of the five computers. Sand covered the floor.

Stan sat down on a big beach chair in front of one of the computers. "Give me the key," he said. "I want to take a digital photo of it so I can show it to some people."

I pulled the key out of my pocket and handed it to Stan. He placed it on his desk, then pulled a silver camera from a drawer. He aimed at the key and clicked the shutter. But there was no flash. No sound at all. "Did the camera work?" I asked.

"Sure, little dude. Watch," Stan answered. He

hooked the camera up to his computer. In a moment, a picture of the key appeared on the screen. Cool.

I glanced around the office. I couldn't stop staring at all the props Stan had set up. We should decorate one of the guest bedrooms at the hotel like this, I thought.

"Is this guy really a surfer?" I whispered to Nick.

"Stan hates the water," Nick whispered back. "He only surfs the Net."

"Okay, I'm going into one of the chat rooms. It's a place where dudes into paranormal stuff hang out," Stan announced. "Cool! My friend Casper is here! Now I'm telling everyone in the chat room to look at the picture of the key."

"Stan thinks maybe you and Howie were using the key wrong," Nick explained. "That could be why the spells kept messing up."

"Surf's up!" Stan cried. "Casper says he's heard of the key. He read about a guy who used it to do spells."

"Great!" I exclaimed. "Does he know where the other guy is? Maybe I could talk to him. Maybe he could tell me how to make the key work right."

Stan's fingers flew over the keyboard. "There's a problem," he said. "A big problem. The last guy who used the key has been in an insane asylum for the past fifty years."

Is that what's going to happen to me? I wondered. I could imagine going crazy if I tried too many more spells that didn't work.

"Don't wipe out," Stan told me. "There's someone else who can help you out. Casper says a guy named Mr. Withers would know the secret to using the key."

"Yes!" I cried.

"But there's another problem," Stan said.

"What? Is Mr. Withers in an insane asylum, too?" I demanded. "Maybe I could try to talk to him anyway."

"Uh, no, he's not in an insane asylum," Stan answered.

"That's good," Nick said. "Where is he?"

"Mr. Withers is dead."

Chapter TWELVE

"It wasn't much help," I explained to Grandpa. Nick and I were telling him about our visit to Stan. The three of us sat on a battered couch in the hotel's attic.

I was hiding from my parents. I didn't have time to deal with Dad's questions or Mom's panic. I had to figure out how to stop shrinking—now.

I'd shrunk down to the size of an eight-year-old— and was getting shorter by the minute.

"There are only two people who know about the key," I went on. "One guy's in an insane asylum. Then there's some guy named Mr. Withers. He's dead."

Grandpa stroked his long gray mustache. "I've heard of Mr. Withers," he said.

"As the story goes, more than a hundred years

ago, Mr. Withers used to work for Simon Fear," Grandpa continued. "He lived right here in this house—it used to be part of the Fear estate."

"What did he do for Mr. Fear?" Nick asked.

"He managed Simon Fear's business affairs," Grandpa answered. "But there were rumors. Some people said Simon Fear had a laboratory in his mansion where he did strange experiments. They said that Mr. Withers's *real* job was to assist him in the lab."

"Why are we even talking about this?" I burst out. "Mr. Withers is dead. Even if he did know how to use the key, he can't help me now! He's dead!"

"That's not necessarily true," Grandpa said. "When I was a little boy and I had a problem, my grandmother always said I should go dig up Mr. Withers."

"Huh?" I shook my head.

"I never did it. I thought it was just a story. But my grandmother said that Mr. Withers wasn't quite dead," Grandpa explained. "She said if I dug him up and gave him a drink of water, he would sit up in his coffin and talk to me."

"You've got to try it," Nick said. "You've got to ask Mr. Withers how to use the key the right way."

I shoved up my sleeves. My clothes were getting too big for me. "Do you really think this crazy story is true?" I asked.

"I know my grandparents thought so," Grandpa

answered. "Whenever my grandmother mentioned Mr. Withers, my grandfather would tell her to be quiet. He said it was bad luck even to speak Mr. Withers's name."

My shrinking body shuddered. I didn't like the sound of this. Not at all.

"Do it, Joe. What choice do you have?" Nick said. "I'll go with you."

At least I won't have to dig up a dead guy all by myself, I thought. That would be totally creepy.

"No, Joe *has* to do it alone," Grandpa replied. "My grandmother said if you want to talk to Mr. Withers, you have to go alone—and you have to go at midnight."

I rubbed my arms with my hands. Suddenly, it felt cold in the attic.

"I'll go tonight," I said. My voice shook a little. I hoped Nick didn't notice. "Do you know which cemetery Mr. Withers is buried in?"

"He's not buried in either cemetery. They wouldn't take him," Grandpa answered. "People thought . . . they thought Mr. Withers was evil. Pure evil. They said he never broke a promise—but his promises were horrible. Once he promised to gouge someone's eyes out—and he did it. People didn't want him buried in the same ground with their friends and relatives."

And I'm supposed to ask him for help? I thought.

"Where *is* Mr. Withers buried?" Nick asked.

Grandpa stared down at the floor for a moment. Then he looked up at me. "He's buried in the Fear Street Woods," Grandpa said.

"I have to go into the Fear Street Woods at midnight?" My voice came out in a high squeak.

"Oh, man," Nick mumbled. "Oh, man."

I cleared my throat. "How . . . how am I going to find Mr. Withers's grave?" I asked.

Grandpa hesitated. He didn't want me to go. I could see it in his eyes.

But he knew I had to do it.

"They buried Mr. Withers under a big oak tree," Grandpa answered. "The moment his coffin was covered with earth, the leaves of the tree began dripping blood. They never stopped."

I shone my flashlight over the trees in front of me. All I saw were green leaves.

The woods were so quiet. I could hear the twigs cracking under my feet and the sound of my shovel dragging across the ground.

But I didn't hear anything else—no animals moving around, and definitely no other people.

Robin and Liz, the girls from the Monster Club, said that no birds lived in the Fear Street Woods. Maybe it's true, I thought. Otherwise I should hear an owl hooting once in a while.

Do the birds know something I don't? I wondered. Do they know it's a bad idea to be in these woods?

All I wanted to do was find Mr. Withers's grave and get out of there. I started walking faster.

My shoes felt loose on my feet—even though I was wearing a pair I had already outgrown. And my pants were dragging on the ground—even though I had cut several inches off the bottom before I left the house.

I knelt down and rolled up the cuffs of my pants. The skin of my legs felt loose and rubbery. Then I heard a sucking sound. My skin rippled—then tightened up with a snap.

What just happened? I rubbed the skin. It felt normal.

I must be shrinking faster on the *inside*. That's what made my skin feel so loose. Then it shrank down to fit my smaller body.

I hadn't even thought about what was happening to the inside of my body. My heart, and stomach, and everything must be shrinking, too.

I pushed myself to my feet and started to run. I had to find Mr. Withers—now!

If I didn't, I would totally disappear. Vanish. I'd never see my parents, or Neddy, or Grandpa again. I felt my throat tighten.

I passed tree after tree. More green leaves.

What was I going to do? Time was running out. I

had to find Mr. Withers tonight. If I didn't, it might be too late.

Drip, drip, drip.

Just what I needed. Rain.

But I didn't feel any raindrops. Where was that sound coming from?

Drip, drip, drip.

It's the blood! I realized. It's the sound of the blood dripping off Mr. Withers's tree!

I raced toward the sound. I burst into a clearing and skidded to a stop. In the center of the clearing stood a huge oak tree. The leaves glistened with wet blood.

Drip, drip, drip.

I couldn't move. All I could do was stare. Drops of the blood fell off the leaves and stained the ground red.

I slowly walked toward the tree. The muddy ground slid under my feet. I'm stepping in the blood, I thought. I felt my stomach cramp.

I wanted to get out of there. But didn't see a head-stone or anything. Where was I supposed to dig? Pick a spot, any spot, I told myself.

I stuck my flashlight in my backpack. Then I grabbed the shovel with both hands.

I took a deep breath—and started to dig.

Chapter THIRTEEN

The shovel was hard to use. It wasn't made for someone as short as me.

But I kept digging—deeper and deeper. Nothing there. I tried a different spot. Still nothing. I realized it could take days to dig holes all the way around the tree. And time was running out. But I couldn't give up.

I thrust the shovel into the dirt again—and hit something hard. Yes!

I grabbed the flashlight out of my backpack. I shone it into the hole. I could see something wooden down there.

Mr. Withers's coffin!

I had seen coffins before. We had a few decorating the hotel. But it was a lot different seeing a coffin when you knew there was someone dead inside.

I'd never seen a dead body before. I never *wanted* to see one.

My stomach cramped up again. My heart was racing. I took a deep, shaky breath and forced myself to keep digging.

I put the flashlight away. I had to do this. I shoveled the dirt off the coffin as fast as I could.

Now I had to get the lid open. I stretched out on my stomach next to the grave. I could feel the front of my shirt getting wet. It was starting to stick to my skin. It's the blood, I realized. That blood is getting all over me!

I shuddered. Don't think about it, I told myself. I reached into the grave. But I couldn't touch the top of the coffin.

I wriggled forward and tried again. But I still wasn't close enough. I'm going to have to go in, I realized.

I shoved myself to my feet. I stared into the grave for a moment—then jumped.

Thump! I landed on the coffin. Does Mr. Withers know I'm up here? I wondered.

I hoped not.

I scrambled off the lid and crouched next to the coffin. I ran my fingers along the side. I felt a latch near the center. I gave it a tug. It didn't budge.

It's rusted shut, I decided. I jerked on the latch with both hands. Come on, come on! I thought. It slid open with a squeak.

Am I just supposed to yank up the lid? I thought. That seemed kind of rude. And I definitely didn't want to make Mr. Withers mad at me.

I knocked lightly on the top of the coffin. "Um, hello?" I called. No one answered.

I positioned my hands on the lid. My fingers shook so hard it was difficult to keep my grip on the wood. "Here goes," I whispered.

I pulled open the lid of the coffin and stared down at Mr. Withers's face. I felt a cold chill slide through my body. A low moan escaped from my lips.

Mr. Withers's eye sockets were filled with squirming white maggots. They ate his eyes, I realized. I could imagine them nibbling on the soft, tender flesh.

Half of Mr. Withers's nose was gone. They probably ate that, too, I thought.

There was a hole in Mr. Withers's cheek that went all the way down to the bone. Spongy gray stuff spilled out of a hole in his forehead.

That gray stuff is his brain, I realized. The maggots have been feeding on his brain!

I have to get out of here! I can't do this! I started to slam the coffin shut. Then I noticed how loose the skin on my hands looked. My insides were shrinking again.

I heard the little sucking sound—and my skin

tightened up.

That's it. I have to do this.

I slid my fingers between Mr. Withers's lips and pried open his mouth. I tried not to touch Mr. Withers's tongue. It looked diseased. White splotches covered it.

Those are maggots! I realized. I jerked my hand away. I shone my flashlight over my fingers. Did I get any on me? I did not want one maggot touching me. I'd already seen what they did to Mr. Withers.

I wiped my sweaty hands on my shirt and pulled a bottle of water out of my backpack. I used my teeth to pull off the top. My hands still hadn't stopped shaking.

I poured some of the water into Mr. Withers's mouth. I heard a gurgling sound as it ran down the man's throat. A little stream poured out of a maggot hole in his neck.

I kept my eyes locked on Mr. Withers's face. Was anything happening?

I leaned closer. Was he breathing?

Mr. Withers remained motionless.

I leaned a little closer.

Mr. Withers sat up fast. His hands shot out. They closed around my throat—and began to squeeze.

Chapter FOURTEEN

I struggled to pull in a breath.

Mr. Withers's fingers squeezed tighter and tighter.

My vision blurred. I'm going to pass out, I thought.

"Mooore," Mr. Withers moaned. "Moooore."

"What?" I screamed. My voice came out in a croak. "I don't know what you want." Mr. Withers's fingernails bit into my skin.

Mr. Withers shook me. His head snapped back and forth. "Mooore waaater."

More water! I poured the rest of the water into Mr. Withers's mouth. "Here, take it. You can have it all," I gasped. "Please, just let me go."

Mr. Withers released his grip on my neck. I sucked in a gulp of air. Then another. My lungs felt as if they were on fire.

"Who are you?" Mr. Withers demanded. Squirming

maggots spilled from his mouth with each word. They fell onto his chest with tiny plopping sounds.

"I . . . uh . . . my name is Joe Turner," I stammered. I pushed myself as far away from Mr. Withers as I could. The dirt wall of the grave crumbled under my back. "I need your help."

Mr. Withers stared at me with his blank eyes. "Why would I wish to help you?" he asked.

Why would he? I had no idea. I shouldn't have come here. Vanishing might be okay. Anything would be better than staring down at Mr. Withers's decaying face.

"My grandfather said you would talk to anyone who gave you a drink of water," I said as fast as I could. "I just want to ask you a question. It will take only a second. I promise."

"The water was very refreshing. I haven't had a drink in years," Mr. Withers answered. He smoothed the lapels of his black suit. "Ask your question."

I can't believe this, I thought. Grandpa was right! It's working!

I didn't know whether to be glad—or scared to death.

I pulled the key out of my pocket. Try and act normal, I coached myself. Don't let Mr. Withers know you're afraid. "I want to know how to use this," I said.

Mr. Withers took the key from me. He turned it

over in his hands. "I haven't seen this in years. I made it for my apprentice. It gave him the extra power he needed to perform the more difficult spells."

He shook his head. "The poor boy. He was murdered. His killer set him on fire and burned him to death," Mr. Withers said. "Whoever killed him stole the key."

Mr. Withers peered at me. "How did you come to have it?"

I didn't want to tell Mr. Withers that my ancestor Colin Fear was the one who stole the key. Mr. Withers wouldn't be too happy to hear that one of my relatives killed his apprentice.

I rubbed my throat. I could still feel the places where Mr. Withers's fingers had dug into me.

"Um, my grandfather found the key in the canvas of an old painting," I answered. That was the truth. It just wasn't the *whole* truth.

"I used that key to do four spells," I continued. "It sort of worked. But it made bad stuff happen, too," I explained. "It made me switch bodies with my grandfather. And it made my grandpa disappear. And now it's making me shrink."

Mr. Withers laughed. He laughed, and laughed, and laughed.

The sound made my teeth hurt. "It's not funny!" I cried. "If I keep shrinking, I'm going to disappear!"

Mr. Withers laughed harder. A chunk of the spongy gray stuff fell out of the hole in his forehead. It landed on his white shirt with a splat.

I couldn't believe it. This guy was totally not going to help me! I stumbled to my feet. I struggled to climb up the side of the grave.

Mr. Withers grabbed me by the foot and jerked me back down. I landed on my knees next to the coffin. "Leave me alone!" I shrieked.

"I know the secret of the key. I know how it works," Mr. Withers said calmly. "I'll tell you what you need to know."

"Really?" I asked. Could I believe Mr. Withers?

"I see no reason not to," Mr. Withers answered. "I have no other pressing appointments." He scratched his ear—and it fell off.

Eeew. I tried to steady my stomach. But my supper kept threatening to come up.

I tried not to act grossed out. I didn't want to do anything that might set Mr. Withers off. "Thank you so, so much," I said.

Mr. Withers held up both hands. "Not so fast," he answered. "I will share the secret of the key with you. But first I need you to do a small favor for me."

"A small favor?" I repeated. I heard my voice trembling.

Please let it be very small, I thought.

"I haven't been outside this coffin for more than a

hundred years," Mr. Withers told me. "I want to go into town. I want to see what Shadyside has become."

That's not too bad, I thought.

"I could show you around," I answered. I thought going into town was a good idea. I'd be a lot safer there. At least if I screamed for help, someone might hear me. "I haven't lived here that long, but—"

"No, no, no," Mr. Withers interrupted. "The only way I can leave my coffin is if I find a replacement."

"A replacement?" I repeated.

Please don't let that mean what I think it means, I thought.

"That's right. If you stay in my coffin, I can leave and go into town. I wouldn't stay long—just until dawn," Mr. Withers said. "And when I get back, I'll tell you exactly how the key works."

I glanced at my watch. It wasn't even one yet. There were hours to go before dawn.

"Do we have a deal?" Mr. Withers asked. He held out his hand.

What choice do I have? I thought. I didn't have time to try and find another way to stop shrinking.

"We have a deal," I answered. I reached out to shake on it.

I heard a cracking sound—and one of Mr. Withers's fingers broke off in my hand.

Chapter FIFTEEN

"**O**h, uh, sorry," I mumbled. I handed Mr. Withers back his finger.

"One of the problems of getting old," Mr. Withers said. "Maybe I'll be able to locate a needle and thread in town. I can just stitch it back on."

Mr. Withers stood up in the coffin. He gave a little hop and hooked his arms over the edge of the grave. He hauled himself up to the ground.

"Climb on in there, young man," he called.

I checked the bottom of the coffin for maggots. I didn't spot any, so I stepped inside. "I don't have to lie down, do I?" I asked.

"No, no," Mr. Withers answered. "And you may leave the lid open. The only thing you must do is remain in the coffin until I return at dawn. If you don't, our deal is broken."

Mr. Withers gave me a little wave and headed across the clearing.

I pulled my flashlight out of my backpack. I turned in a slow circle. I shone the beam upward toward the rim of the grave.

You're okay, I told myself. Nothing bad is going to happen to you.

I couldn't stop thinking about the stories I had heard about the Fear Street Woods.

First, there was the story about how no birds lived there. But that was only the beginning.

All the Monster Club members knew a lot about Fear Street. Robin said that weird shadow monsters lived in the caves at the edge of the woods.

I made another slow circle. I saw a lot of shadows. But they looked like regular, normal shadows. And they weren't moving toward me or anything.

Another story popped into my mind. Johnny told me how the whole Monster Club caught a werewolf in the woods one night when the moon was full.

I checked the sky. Good. The moon wasn't full tonight.

Grandpa had some stories about the woods, too. He said that there was some kind of creature living at the bottom of Fear Lake. It drowned anyone who dared to swim in its water.

I bet the creature can't survive on dry land, I told

myself. I took another look around the clearing—just to be sure.

I felt a little better. Then I remembered what Liz told me. She said sometimes the kids in Shadyside played hide-and-seek in the woods—with a ghost. If the ghost tagged a kid, it got to take over the kid's body.

I knew how that felt. The ghost that haunted me, Martin Jackson, had control of my body for a while. He tried to make me kill myself. Then Grandpa used a spell to banish Martin.

That was the spell that made me and Grandpa switch bodies. That's how I ended up here—standing in a coffin in the Fear Street Woods, I thought.

I started to make another slow circle. I swung the flashlight from side to side. I wanted to see as much as possible.

There's nothing out there, I told myself. And even if there *is* something out there, the light will keep it away.

Yeah, I'm okay, I thought. As long as I have this flashlight, I'm safe.

My flashlight flickered.

Then it went out—leaving me in total darkness.

Chapter SIXTEEN

I shook the flashlight. I switched it off, then switched it back on again.

But it didn't help.

Was something creeping up on me now that the light was out? Something I couldn't see?

I peered into the darkness. It's hopeless, I thought. By the time I spot something, it will be practically on top of me.

I sat down in the coffin. Maybe the grave would give me a little protection. Maybe no one—or nothing—would notice me in the hole.

And maybe there is nothing out there in the woods at all, I thought. Maybe all the stories about the Fear Street Woods are just *stories*.

I heard the soft sucking sound and felt the skin of

my neck grow tighter. What if I shrink so fast I'm not even here when Mr. Withers gets back? I thought.

I checked my watch. It was almost one-thirty.

Maybe Mr. Withers will get bored and come back early. There's not much to do in Shadyside in the middle of the night.

Yeah, right, I told myself. Mr. Withers's coffin is *much* more exciting.

I had to face facts. Mr. Withers would not come back one second before dawn.

I held my watch close to my eyes. I saw the second hand go around, and around, and around.

I yawned. And yawned again. My eyelids felt heavy.

But I couldn't go to sleep. It would be too dangerous to fall asleep in the Fear Street Woods. Way too dangerous.

Maybe doing the multiplication tables would help me stay awake. "Two times two is four," I whispered. "Two times three is six. Two times four is eight."

I yawned. My mouth stretched open so wide my jaws cracked.

"Two . . . times . . . five . . . is . . . ten," I said. My words came out more and more slowly.

"Two . . . times . . . six . . . is . . . is . . . is . . ."

The multiplication tables aren't helping, I

thought. They're making me even sleepier!

I pinched myself—hard.

I could try to figure out how much I'm shrinking every hour, I thought.

No. That might keep me awake. But it would also scare me to death!

I know! I'll make a list of all the mean tricks David Sutherland played on me. David was this kid at my old school. He was a total bully.

Thinking about David won't scare me. It will make me mad. And when I'm mad, I never feel sleepy.

Okay, what is the very first mean trick I remember? I asked myself.

I stretched out in the coffin and rested my head on the little satin pillow. The soft, soft pillow.

There was that time David told me everyone in the third grade always wore their bathing suits to the first day of school, I thought.

I closed my eyes.

I'm just going to rest them for a minute. I'm not going to sleep or anything.

Then there was the time David . . . the time David . . .

Crack!

My eyes snapped open.

What was that?

Crack!

It sounded like a twig snapping. And that meant

someone or some*thing* was moving around in the clearing.

I sat up fast.

Crack! Crunch! Crack!

And it's getting closer! I thought.

It's coming toward me!

Chapter SEVENTEEN

I scrambled to my feet—and saw Mr. Withers hurrying toward me.

I let out a long, shaky breath. I couldn't believe it. Mr. Withers came back early!

I survived my night in the Fear Street Woods, I thought. Now I can find out the secret to using the key and go home!

"Hey, how did you like Shadyside? Was it a lot different than you remembered it? Did you have fun? What did you do?" I called. I couldn't stop babbling. I was so happy to see Mr. Withers!

Mr. Withers didn't answer any of my questions. He rushed up to the edge of the grave.

Then he grabbed my shovel.

My heart started to pound. "What are you doing with that?" I cried.

Wham! A shovelful of dirt hit me in the face.

I staggered backward. The dirt burned my eyes. I used my sleeve to wipe it away.

"I know we had a deal, and I do apologize for breaking it," Mr. Withers said. He threw another shovelful of dirt down on me. "But I experienced such wonderful things tonight."

"Nooo!" I howled. I hurled myself at the top of the grave. But it was too high.

Mr. Withers shoveled faster and faster. "Wonderful, wonderful things," he repeated.

I leaped into the air again. I couldn't reach the top.

I'm too short, I realized. I'm never going to make it.

"I ate my first microwaved burrito and drank my first cherry slushie," Mr. Withers said as he shoveled. "True delicacies, Joe."

I spotted a long root about halfway up the wall. I can use that to pull myself up, I thought. I'm getting out of here! I am!

I bent my knees—and leaped toward the root. I caught it in both hands. Yes!

"I saw people riding in carriages made of steel," Mr. Withers continued. He kept shoveling. "Carriages that didn't need horses to pull them."

I ignored him. I used the root like a rope. I crawled up it hand over hand.

I'm halfway there, I thought. I hooked one arm over the edge of the grave. I dug my fingers into the ground, anchoring myself.

"No, you don't," Mr. Withers screeched. "I'm not going back. There are too many wonderful things to see."

He slammed his foot down on my hand.

I cried out in pain, and lost my grip.

Thud! I fell flat on my back in the coffin.

Slam! Mr. Withers used the shovel to close the lid.

I heard a clump of dirt hit the lid of the coffin. Then another.

Mr. Withers was burying me alive!

Chapter EIGHTEEN

"Let me out!" I shouted. I slammed my fists into the lid of the coffin.

It didn't move.

My muscles have been shrinking, too, I realized. I have puny little arms now. I'm too weak to get out of here.

Thump! Thump! Thump!

Shovelfuls of dirt fell on the lid of the coffin.

I can't just lie here and let him bury me, I thought. I have to fight back.

I bent my knees toward my chest and pressed my feet against the lid. There were some advantages to being small. I had room to maneuver inside the coffin.

One, two, three—go! I kicked with both legs as hard as I could.

Bang! The coffin lid flew open.

"Yes!" I shouted. A clump of dirt landed in my mouth.

I spit it out and jumped to my feet. I scrambled on top of the open edge of the coffin lid.

I balanced for a moment on the narrow piece of wood. Then I threw myself at the top of the grave.

Mr. Withers gave a high scream of fury. He aimed a kick at me.

I grabbed him by the foot—and we tumbled back into the coffin together.

I was smaller—and faster. I scrambled out of the coffin and slammed the lid shut.

"Now I have *you* trapped!" I yelled.

The coffin lid jerked underneath me. Mr. Withers was bigger—and stronger. And he wanted out.

I threw myself facedown on the coffin. I had to close the latch before Mr. Withers escaped.

I ran my fingers along the side of the coffin. I felt the thick metal latch. "Now I've got you," I muttered.

Mr. Withers shoved on the coffin lid again. It jerked open a few inches—and Mr. Withers shot his hand out. He grabbed me by the wrist.

I tried to jerk away, but Mr. Withers's bony fingers held tight. They dug into my skin, and I gave a yelp of pain.

Suddenly I remembered the way one of Mr.

Withers's fingers fell off when we shook hands. That's it! I thought.

I used my free hand to grab Mr. Withers's pinky finger. Snap! I broke it off.

Snap! Snap! Snap! Snap! Four more fingers gone.

"Noooo! I forgot to get a needle and thread!" Mr. Withers wailed. He jerked his mangled hand back inside the coffin.

I slammed the latch shut.

"Let me out!" Mr. Withers cried. His voice was muffled by the coffin, but I could still hear him.

"That's what *I* said," I shot back. "But you didn't listen to me—so I'm not listening to you."

I slammed my fist down on the coffin. "We had a deal and you cheated!" I shouted. "I thought you never broke a promise."

"You're right," Mr. Withers answered. "It was dishonorable of me. The world is just such an amazing place. I couldn't bear to give it up."

Mr. Withers gave a long, loud sigh. "I'll tell you what you want to know now."

Is he trying to trick me? I wondered. Or is he serious?

"You'll have to tell me from inside the coffin," I said. "There is no way I'm letting you out again."

"Fair enough, young man," Mr. Withers answered. "As I said, I made the key for my apprentice—and only my apprentice can safely use it."

"What?" I cried.

"I didn't want the key to fall into the wrong hands," Mr. Withers continued. "I put an enchantment on it. If anyone but my apprentice tried to use it, they would bring destruction on themselves."

"And that's why my spells kept making bad things happen to me," I said.

"Yes," Mr. Withers replied. "I used a very powerful enchantment. One of my best."

"You have to fix the key so it will work for me," I said. "We can make a new bargain. I'll bring you tons of burritos and slushies and lots of other cool stuff. Just please take off the enchantment."

"I wish I could," Mr. Withers told me. "But the only person who can help you is my apprentice."

"But he must be dead, too," I said.

Mr. Withers snorted. "Surely at your age you have learned how to call up a spirit."

"Yeah," I answered. "I've done that before."

Nick and I and the rest of the Monster Club did a seance. That's how Martin Jackson's ghost was released in the first place.

"Then you have your solution," Mr. Withers said. "Call up the spirit of my apprentice and he will help you."

"Thanks," I called. "I, uh, have to go now. Bye."

"You're welcome, Joe," Mr. Withers called back.

"Oh," I remembered. "I need to know the name of

90

your apprentice, so I can call him up."

"Of course," Mr. Withers answered. "You'll like him. He was always a good boy."

Cool, I thought. Maybe my luck really *is* starting to change.

"My apprentice's name is Martin Jackson," Mr. Withers continued.

My heart sank. Oh, no! The ghost of Martin Jackson would definitely *not* want to help me.

Martin Jackson thought I was his killer. Martin Jackson wanted me dead!

Chapter NINETEEN

I swung the front door open and crept inside.

Grandpa rushed up to me. "What happened?" he cried. "Did you find Mr. Withers?"

I gently closed the door behind me. "Shhh. Don't wake up Mom and Dad," I said.

Nick burst into the hall. "What took so long? We were about to come after you!"

"Hey, what are you still doing here?" I asked Nick.

"I thought you might need backup," he said. "I told my mom I was sleeping over because we had a big oral report to work on."

Wow, what a cool thing to do, I thought. Nick and I had met each other only a few weeks ago—and Nick was already a great friend.

"Thanks," I mumbled.

"So what happened?" Grandpa demanded.

"I'll tell you the whole story later—when I'm not shrinking," I answered. "The important thing is that I found out what we have to do to make the key work right."

"What?" Nick exclaimed.

"We have to have another seance," I said. "We have to call up the spirit of Martin Jackson again."

Nick's eyes opened wide. Grandpa's face went pale.

"Martin almost killed you the last time," Grandpa reminded me. I could tell he was trying really hard to keep calm.

"He tried to make you stab yourself with a saber," Grandpa continued. "And he almost made you walk off the roof!"

"Mr. Withers said Martin is the only one who can use the key. We don't have any choice. We have to call him back here. I'll just—find a way to handle him," I insisted.

"There's something you have to know," Nick said. "I read a book about seances. It said that each time you summon a spirit, it grows stronger."

Nick swallowed hard. "That means that this time Martin is going to be even more powerful!"

Chapter TWENTY

"**T**hanks for coming over in the middle of the night," I said. "I couldn't wait until tomorrow to do the seance. I'm shrinking so fast, I might not be here!"

I tugged on the end of my T-shirt. It was one of Neddy's—and it was already a little too long.

"Hey, we're the Monster Club," Robin answered. "It's what we do."

"Besides, it gave us a chance to try out our emergency broadcast system," Johnny added.

"We can send out alarms to each other by e-mail," Liz explained. "We rigged our computers so a beep goes off when it's an emergency."

"You'll have to remember to leave your computer on at night from now on, Joe," Robin said.

Joining the Monster Club was the smartest thing I

ever did, I thought. When you live on Fear Street, it's good to have friends who know about monsters, and ghosts, and seances, and stuff.

"Okay, let's do it," Nick said. "Is everyone clear on the new way to do the seance? It's supposed to give us more control over the spirit. If Martin does come back even stronger, we're going to need all the help we can get."

Johnny, Robin, Liz, and I nodded. Nick handed us each a thick purple candle. He lit the flames—then he clicked off the lights.

I sat down on the living room floor and placed my candle in front of me. The others sat down, too. We formed a tight circle with the candles in the middle.

Robin glanced over at me. "Your parents aren't going to wake up and come downstairs, are they?" she asked. "This is definitely *not* something adults would understand."

"Grandpa is keeping watch at the top of the stairs. He's cool. He won't let anyone down here until we're done," I answered.

Liz sat next to me, and I had to tilt my head back to look her in the eye. It felt so weird to be shorter than Liz. She was the shortest kid in the Monster Club. She was the shortest kid in my *whole* class.

Now she looks big enough to be my baby-sitter, I thought.

"Okay, let's go." Nick cleared his throat. "Martin

Jackson, we call on the power of earth to summon you."

He pulled a pinch of dirt out of his pocket and sprinkled it over the candles. The flames blazed brighter. A line of purple smoke drifted up from each candle.

I heard Johnny draw in a long breath. He's nervous, I realized. But he can't be as nervous as I am. My life depends on this seance working.

"Martin Jackson, we call on the power of water to summon you," Brian said. His voice cracked a little.

He reached into his pocket and pulled out a squirt gun. He sprayed the water over the candles. They sputtered, flickered, then burned brighter than before.

The four lines of purple smoke twisted together. They formed one thick column.

I squeezed my eyes shut. This is too weird, I thought.

"Martin Jackson, we call on the power of air to summon you," I heard Robin say.

Don't be a chicken, I thought. I forced myself to open my eyes. I watched as Robin leaned toward the candles and blew gently across the flames.

The flames doubled in size. The column of smoke grew taller and thicker.

I thought I saw something forming in the column. Something with eyes.

What is that? Is it him—Martin?

Nick nudged me in the ribs. Oh, right, I thought. It's my turn.

"Martin Jackson, we call on the power of fire to summon you," I said firmly.

I reached behind me and grabbed a thick red candle. I placed it in the center of the circle with the others.

Nick handed me a matchbook. I almost dropped it. My fingers were slick with sweat.

I stretched out my hand and lit the red candle. The candles popped and sparked.

Liz gasped as the column of smoke turned red.

A high whining sound filled the room—and the column of smoke began to spin. It whirled faster and faster—forming a miniature tornado.

My hair whipped across my face. I shoved it out of my eyes and stared at the tornado.

I saw the flash of a hand inside it. Then a glimpse of hair. A leg. And the eyes again.

"There is something alive in there," Johnny cried.

The whining sound stopped abruptly. The tornado stopped spinning.

The smoke turned back to purple. It slowly drifted away—and I saw a boy floating over the candles. It was him. The ghost. Martin Jackson.

I dug my fingernails into my palms to keep from screaming.

I could hardly stand to look at Martin's face.

Burns covered his skin. Oozing burns. The burns went so deep that I could see patches of muscle and pieces of white bone.

And his eyes. I shuddered.

One of Martin's eyes was swollen shut. And the other . . . the other hung from its socket by a bloody thread.

"Can he see us?" Robin whispered.

Martin's eye twitched. It moved toward her, pulling on the thread of muscle that held it in place.

Martin's mouth slowly opened. "Who are you?" he croaked. "Why have you summoned me?"

Nick was right about the new seance giving us more control, I realized. Martin seemed really confused. He acted as if he didn't know where he was. And he hadn't even noticed me yet.

Good, I thought. This will give us a chance to talk to him. We can explain everything. Maybe this time Martin will believe that I'm really not Colin Fear.

"We summoned you because we need your help," Nick said.

Thanks for saying we, I thought. My friends were definitely with me one hundred percent.

Martin's eye turned toward Nick.

"We used your key to do a spell. Something bad happened." Nick spoke faster and faster. "My friend Joe started to shrink. He will disappear if you don't use the key to reverse the spell. You're the only one who can do it."

Martin's eye shot closer to Nick—it stopped less than an inch away from Nick's face. The eye studied Nick for a long while.

Nick stared back without blinking.

Whoa, I thought. I don't know if I could do that.

"You have my key?" Martin asked. "Let me see it."

I pulled the key out of my pocket and held it up. "Here it is."

Martin stretched his eye toward the key. Then he moved it up to my face.

"Colin Fear!" he screeched. "You killed me for that key—and now I am going to kill you!"

Chapter TWENTY-ONE

"I'm *not* Colin!" I cried. "Colin died almost a hundred years ago."

Martin's mouth opened in a howl of fury. He curled his fingers into claws and flew at me.

I scrambled away—and my back slammed into the coffee table. He's got me!

Nick yanked off one of his sneakers and hurled it at Martin's head. *Wham!*

Martin spun away from me and advanced on Nick.

"See that shoe?" Nick demanded. "They didn't have anything like that when you were alive."

Robin leaned close to me. "Time for the plan. Go!" she whispered.

I slowly pushed myself to my feet. I didn't want Martin to see me.

"You've been dead for a hundred years," Nick continued.

"Yeah. And that means Colin Fear has to be dead, too," Brian jumped in.

I crept out of the room. I tiptoed down the hall to the front door. I slipped outside. I didn't close the door behind me. I didn't want to risk making the tiniest sound.

Okay, now run! I ordered myself.

I raced across the front yard—and took off down the street. I pumped my short legs as hard as I could.

Martin's going to fly after me any second, I thought.

My feet slid back and forth in my shoes as I ran. I was already too small for them. I stopped and yanked them off. They were slowing me down—and every second counted now.

"*You won't escape me this time, Colin Fear,*" Martin's voice bellowed from behind me.

I knew it. He's already outside, I thought. How close is he?

I didn't stop to look. I knew Martin was way too close—wherever he was.

"Look at this, Martin," I heard Liz yell. She must have chased Martin out of the house, I thought. "It's a calculator. You didn't have one of these when you were alive. They weren't invented yet."

"This time you die, Colin Fear."

Martin sounded closer.

They aren't going to be able to stop him again, I thought. But I have one more chance—if I can get to the cemetery before Martin does.

I could see the cemetery's iron fence in the distance. I tried to pick up speed. But my little legs and feet couldn't take very big steps.

"Now I have you, Colin Fear."

Martin screamed the words in my ear.

I felt hands grab the back of my T-shirt—then my feet left the ground.

"Wha—?" I exclaimed. I looked down—and my heart froze in my chest. Martin had pulled me into the air.

Martin gave a screech of triumph as he pulled me higher and higher.

Farther from the ground.

Chapter TWENTY-TWO

"**P**ut me down!" I screamed. I jerked my body back and forth. I tried to twist out of Martin's grasp.

But Martin held on tight. He shot higher into the air. Higher than the street signs. Higher than the houses.

This is how Martin plans to kill me! I thought. He's going to haul me way, way up in the air—and drop me.

My heart beat so hard, I could hear it. It pounded in my ears.

Any second Martin would let go—and I would plunge to the ground. I could already feel my soft body smashing into the hard cement of the side-walk.

I glanced down. A wave of dizziness swept through me.

I squeezed my eyes shut. I couldn't watch. I didn't want to know how high we were.

I felt the air rush by my face as Martin whooshed up and up and up. Something rough scraped my face, and the scent of pine needles filled my nose.

My eyes flew open. I saw the branches of a huge pine tree flying past me.

I shot out my hands and grabbed one of the branches. I jerked myself toward the trunk and wrapped both my legs around it.

"Nooo!" Martin howled.

I pressed myself closer to the tree. I wrapped my arms around the trunk. I dug my fingernails into the rough bark.

Martin gave the back of my T-shirt a hard yank.

My head snapped back. I bit my tongue and tasted blood in my mouth.

Before I could recover, Martin jerked me again.

One of my fingernails ripped free. Pain shot up my arm. My grip loosened.

Martin shook me back and forth. He whipped me from side to side.

I grunted as I struggled to keep my grip on the tree. "Don't let go. Don't let go. Don't let go," I chanted to myself.

But Martin was too strong. I felt my hands slipping away from the trunk.

Martin uttered a long shriek of laughter.

I'm not giving up, I thought. No way.

Martin gave another yank on the back of my T-shirt. I held on to the trunk tightly with my legs. I lifted my hands over my head—and let Martin pull the shirt off me.

Martin shot into the air, carrying the shirt.

Yes! I scrambled down the tree. As soon as I was low enough, I jumped to the ground.

I have to get to the cemetery before Martin grabs me again, I thought. I have to go with the backup plan the Monster Club came up with. It was my only shot at surviving.

I tore down the sidewalk. I tripped on the cuff of one of my pant legs. I fell to my knees.

Oh, no! I'm still shrinking!

A whistling sound met my ears. I jerked my head up—and saw Martin dive-bombing straight toward me.

I threw myself down on the ground and rolled. Martin hit the ground with a *thud*.

I didn't look back. I scrambled under a parked car. I took a deep breath and crawled out the other side.

The cemetery gate was only a few feet away. I shoved myself to my feet and dashed over to it.

I grabbed the gate with both hands and pulled. Locked!

But I'm small enough to squeeze through the

bars, I realized. I wriggled between them.

I heard the whistling sound again.

I'm not going to let Martin catch me now, I thought. I'm too close.

I raced into the graveyard, and zigzagged around the tombstones.

I tried to read the headstones as I ran. Where is it? I thought. Where is the grave I need?

There!

I slid to a stop in front of a plain gray gravestone. I turned around and stared up into the sky. Martin was swooping down on me, but he didn't move.

It was time for my last chance. I hoped it would work.

"Look!" I shouted at Martin. I pointed to the tombstone. "This is Colin Fear's grave! He's dead. Dead! I am not Colin Fear—because Colin Fear is *dead*!"

Chapter TWENTY-THREE

Martin stopped in midair. He stared down at me. His eyeball quivered at the end of its thread.

Does he believe me? I thought.

If he doesn't, I'm doomed. He's way too close. I'll never get away if he comes after me now.

"Colin is dead," I repeated. I waved my finger, with its bloody, torn fingernail, in front of Martin. "But I'm alive! Look—I'm bleeding! I'm alive!"

"I'm sorry about what happened to you," I went on. "But I didn't do it. I'm not Colin Fear."

"Colin Fear!" Martin cried. His face twisted in anger—and he swooped down at me.

I threw my arms in front of my face and braced myself. I heard a whistling sound. And I felt air rushing by me.

I flinched. I knew in one second I would feel Martin's hands grab me.

But I didn't. I didn't feel anything. I didn't hear anything. What was going on?

I slowly lowered my arms. I opened my eyes.

Martin knelt on the ground in front of Colin Fear's tombstone. He traced Colin's name with one finger. "He's really dead?"

"Yeah," I answered. "He's been dead for a long, long time. I wish he died even sooner. He deserved it after what he did to you."

Martin stood up. Then he pulled back his foot and kicked Colin's gravestone over. He grinned at me. "That felt good."

"I bet it did." I dug the key out of my pocket. "Here. This belongs to you," I said. I handed it to Martin.

The key began to glow when Martin touched it. It surrounded him with a golden light.

The oozing burns on Martin's face dried up. They grew smaller and lighter until they disappeared.

I heard a sucking sound—then Martin's eye snapped back into its socket.

"Whoa," I muttered.

Martin's other eye opened. The key's golden light dimmed, then went out.

Martin ran his fingers from his forehead to his chin. "I have my face back," he whispered.

"I know that feeling," I said. "One of the spells I did with your key made me switch bodies with my grandpa. I had all these wrinkles, and all this white hair growing out of my ears! I was so happy to get my own body again."

Martin gave a snort of laughter. Then his expression turned serious. "Now a spell is making you shrink. Isn't that what your friend said?"

I nodded.

"Touch the key," Martin said. He held it out, and I touched it lightly.

The key began to glow again. It covered me with its golden light.

My body felt weightless. It's like I'm filled with helium, I thought. I couldn't feel the ground under my feet.

Then the golden light dimmed. I blinked. "Did anything happen?" I mumbled.

"The spell has been reversed," Martin answered.

I stared down at my body. It was back to normal. "Thank you so much," I said.

"I'm sorry I tried to kill you," Martin said. "You look so much like Colin. I was confused."

"It's okay. I probably would have done the same thing if I were you," I said. "So, what are you going to do now? You can still stay at the hotel if you want to. One of our ghost—I mean *guest* rooms is probably free."

Martin shook his head. "Something strange happened when the key was healing me. I heard my mother's voice. She said I was late for dinner. She said I should come home."

"Where's home?" I asked.

"Her voice was coming from over there," Martin said. He pointed deeper into the cemetery. "I'd better go. She hates it when I'm late."

"Yeah, mine does, too," I answered.

Martin took a few steps. He turned and waved at me—and then he disappeared.

"I hope she made your favorite," I said. Then I headed home myself.

"Joe, you're going to be late for school," Mom called.

"I'm leaving right now," I said. I hurried toward the door.

I paused in front of the big hall mirror. I just had to do a quick check.

Yes, I was still the right height. And the right age.

But there was something wrong. My clothes.

I had on jeans and my favorite baseball cap. But my reflection wore goofy knee-length pants and a weird three-cornered hat. Very *old-fashioned* clothes.

I frowned. My reflection smiled.

"We really do look alike," the boy in the mirror

said. "I'm not surprised Martin thought I was you."

Another ghost? One that looked just like me?

No. It couldn't be Colin Fear? I gasped.

"Who else?" the boy asked. "I can't believe you gave my key back to Martin. Do you know how hard it was to steal it from him in the first place?"

R.L. Stine
Seniors
a FEAR STREET series

available from Gold Key® Paperbacks

FEAR STREET® titles
available from Gold Key® Paperbacks:

The Stepbrother
Camp Out
Scream, Jennifer, Scream!
The Bad Girl

FEAR STREET® Sagas
available from Gold Key® Paperbacks:

Circle of Fire
Chamber of Fear
Faces of Terror
One Last Kiss

About R.L. Stine

R.L. Stine is the best-selling author in America. He has written more than one hundred scary books for young people, all of them bestsellers.

His series include *Fear Street, Ghosts of Fear Street,* and the *Fear Street Sagas.*

Bob grew up in Columbus, Ohio. Today he lives in New York City with his wife, Jane, his son, Matt, and his dog, Nadine.